This Little Hippo
book belongs to

_____

_____

For Adam

Scholastic Children's Books
Commonwealth House,
1-19 New Oxford Street, London WC1A 1NU, UK
a division of Scholastic Ltd
London • New York • Toronto • Sydney • Auckland
Mexico City • New Delhi • Hong Kong

First published by Little Hippo, an imprint of Scholastic Ltd, 1999

ISBN 0 590 11416 6

2 4 6 8 10 9 7 5 3 1

Printed in Italy by Amadeus

A PIRATE STORY

Philippa Gregory

Illustrated by Chris Mould

Little Hippo

Our pirate ship, the *Midnight Belle*
was looking a terrible wreck.
The Captain called Bosun and Cabin Boy Dick
and me to parade the deck.

He called us a dastardly desperate crew
and bawled out a long list of things we must do.
"Splice the mainbrace! Launder the sheets!
And then paint the portholes bright blue!
Shiver me timbers! Lock up your chest!
And anything else pirates do!"

We started at lunchtime, the Bosun and me,
with a Yo Ho Ho and Ho.
We thought we'd be finished by quarter to three,
and the Captain would say we could go.

But even by sundown, we'd scarcely begun
with our dusters and mops; and the bottle of rum
didn't help us as much as we thought that it would.
"I hate cleaning!" said Bosun. "I don't see it should

always be my turn. I do my fair share!
Why do I have to? It just isn't fair!"

We were caulking the decks with a cauldron of tar.
It's a job that's terrifically skilled.
It doesn't look much, but goes ever-so-far.
When it accidentally spilled.
I shouted in panic for Cabin Boy Dick,
"Help! Lend a hand! I'm starting to stick!"

Dick came like a whirlwind but in seconds was stuck,
"I can't move an inch! What terrible luck,
but the Bosun will save us. We'll give a loud shout –
how we will laugh when he's pulled us both out!"

Bosun marched over and held out his hand.
"Stop messing about!" was his pirate command.
He pulled me, he skidded, he crashed down on his bum!
So we shouted for Captain. We begged him to come.

He was drinking his cocoa and wasn't best pleased.
"What are you doing? You lumpers! You dolts!
Stuck on the deck by your bottoms and knees!"
"Don't be cross with us Captain! It's none of our faults!"

"And what's all this stuff
that's so sticky and black?"
"Look out, Sir!" we cried.
But too late! He went smack!

Captain blamed Bosun and Bosun blamed me.
The ship sailed itself on the wide empty sea!
Seagulls flew over and poohed on our heads.
The Captain said, "Next time I'll stay in my bed!"
The ship's cat looked snooty and strolled round the rail
Completely unhelpful, she just washed her tail.

We lay there in silence, the full moon rose high
and the wind blew cold 'cross the dark starry sky
and eleven fat treasure ships went sailing by.
They were loaded with diamonds and rubies and gold.
But we didn't care, we were fed-up and cold.

Then it started to rain and the decks got all wet.
So we pulled ourselves up by the ropes and the net
And the tar drained away – at last we were free,
the Captain, the Cabin Boy, Bosun and me!
We were cold, we were hungry, but no longer stuck.
The Cabin Boy said, "At last some good luck!"

"A bath!" said the Captain. "That's what we all need!"
And the Bosun and Cabin Boy sweetly agreed.
I said, "No, thank you! It's not my bath night."
But no-one would listen; so I said, "Oh, all right."

We had a big barrel which we filled to the brim
with hot water and bubbles and the odd shark's fin
to frighten the Cabin Boy, and some bright floating toys,
a couple of ships and a quacky duck noise.

And in we all went, even Primrose the cat,
though her fur went all soggy,
and she didn't like that.
We sang happy songs
and made beards with the bubbles.
We washed off the tar
and forgot all our troubles.

By the time we were dry it was getting near dawn.
I lay back on deck and gave a huge yawn.
The morning sun rose; I was all clean and warm.
Bosun said, "Lemon pancakes? Or kippers and brawn?

Or eggies with soldiers, or porridge and fruit?
Or cornflakes, or kedgeree, baked in a boot?"

I looked at the Bosun and said, "That sounds great!
I'll have the whole lot, if you've got a big plate."
Then I turned to the crew and announced with a grin,
"There's one thing to say, would you like to join in?"

"TAR very much for such lovely big dinners.
We felt very sad till we feasted like winners
and now we don't care that we lost all that treasure.
We'll be jolly pirates for ever and ever!"

Then I asked the Captain, "Please let me steer."
He said that I could, if he stood very near.
"I love being a pirate; and we don't even smell!
We're the cleanest crew ever on the good *Midnight Belle*!"